Who is this cool ghoul?

This really is a mystery, Nancy thought. *Who could the Snowman be?*

Suddenly something big and white dashed out from behind a tree. A bright blue scarf fluttered from its neck as it darted from tree to tree.

"Yikes!" Nancy gasped.

"Nancy—are you okay?" Bess asked.

"Yeah," George said. "You look like you just saw a ghost!"

Join the CLUE CREW
& solve these other cases!

NANCY DREW

AND THE CLUE CREW

#5

Case of the Sneaky Snowman

BY CAROLYN KEENE

ILLUSTRATED BY MACKY PAMINTUAN

Aladdin Paperbacks
New York London Toronto Sydney

🐿 ALADDIN PAPERBACKS

An imprint of Simon & Schuster Children's Publishing Division

1230 Avenue of the Americas, New York, NY 10020

Text copyright © 2006 by Simon & Schuster, Inc.

Illustrations copyright © 2006 by Macky Pamintuan

All rights reserved, including the right of reproduction in whole or in part in any form.

ALADDIN PAPERBACKS, NANCY DREW AND THE CLUE CREW, and colophon are trademarks of Simon & Schuster, Inc.

NANCY DREW is a registered trademark of Simon & Schuster, Inc.

Designed by Lisa Vega

The text of this book was set in ITC Stone Informal.

Manufactured in the United States of America

First Aladdin Paperbacks edition December 2006.

20 19 18 17 16 15 14 13 12

Library of Congress Control Number 2006922340

ISBN-13: 978-1-4169-1254-5

ISBN-10: 1-4169-1254-1

0412 OFF

CONTENTS

CHAPTER ONE

Puzzle in the Park

"And now for the finishing touch!" eight-year-old Nancy Drew said. She held out her hand. "Carrot please, George!"

Nancy's best friend George Fayne dug into the pocket of her bulky blue parka. She pulled out something green and fuzzy. Then she stuck it into the face of the snowman with a *crunch*!

Bess Marvin was Nancy's other best friend. She stared at the fuzzy green thing with wide eyes.

"You were supposed to bring a *carrot* for the snowman's nose," Bess said.

"That's broccoli," Nancy said.

"My mom needed carrots for her catering

1

job," George explained. "Broccoli was the only veggie we had left."

Nancy smiled. It was Tuesday morning and the best winter break ever! That's because it had snowed for two days straight. By the time Nancy, Bess, and George got to the park it looked like a giant marshmallow sundae—perfect for building their first snowman of the year!

"Wait! Wait! We're not finished yet," Bess said. The pom-pom on her red hat bounced as she jumped up and down. "We forgot to *name* our snowman!"

"How about Sherlock?" Nancy asked.

"Sherlock?" George said, wrinkling her nose.

"After Sherlock Holmes, the famous detective in the books," Nancy explained. "We're detectives, so our snowman should have a detective name. Right?"

"Right!" Bess and George said together.

Not only were the girls detectives, but they had their own detective club called the Clue Crew. When a mystery popped up in River Heights, Nancy, Bess, and George were on the case!

The friends stepped back to admire their work. Sherlock had Nancy's old blue scarf wrapped around his neck. Over his head were earmuffs. Bess built them out of two white powder puffs and a plastic headband. George stuck a pair of her dad's old rubber boots near the snowman's base. For his mouth and smile, Nancy used little

3

round dog kibbles—the kind she fed to her puppy, Chocolate Chip.

"Did we do an awesome job or what?" Bess sighed.

"We?" George cried. "You mostly just watched, Bess!"

Bess rubbed her thick red mittens together to keep warm. "I told you. I'm skating in the River Heights Ice Spectacular Show this Saturday," she said. "I can't get my hands cold!"

"You're not skating on your *hands*, Bess," George said. She rolled her dark eyes. "Sometimes I can't believe you're my cousin."

Nancy sometimes couldn't believe it either!

George had dark hair and brown eyes. She was a computer geek and proud of it. Bess had blond hair and blue eyes. She loved building and fixing things. But now Bess had something else to look forward to. A few days ago she won a raffle at the ice-skating rink. The prize was to skate in the ice show with Russian ice dancing stars Svetlana and Alexi Dubonov. On Saturday

4

Bess would wear a pretty costume and ice skates with pink pom-poms. Then she would skate in the show like a star herself!

"It's okay, Bess," Nancy said. "You made Sherlock's earmuffs. That was a big job!"

Bess stuck her chin out at George. Suddenly someone shouted, "Wipeout!"

Nancy, Bess, and George whirled around. A boy was riding a snowboard down the hill—straight toward them! They jumped behind Sherlock and all held their breath as the boy zipped by.

"He almost rode into Sherlock!" George complained.

"And he didn't even say excuse me!" Bess said.

Nancy watched as the boy skidded to a stop at the bottom of the hill. He laughed as he picked up his board and walked away.

"Oh, forget about him," Nancy said. She pulled the zipper of her red parka all the way up to her chin. "Let's go to the Snack Shack for some hot chocolate."

"With marshmallows!" Bess added.

The girls said good-bye to Sherlock. Their boots made deep footprints as they walked through the snowy park. Tons of kids were busy sledding and building snow people. But as the girls passed the playground they saw something that made them stop. Between the slide and the swings was a purple and gold tent!

"That was never there before," Nancy said.

She looked closer. Eight-year-old Toby Leo was standing in front of the tent. Toby was in the girls' third-grade class at River Heights Elementary School. He usually wore a sweatshirt, blue jeans, and sneakers. But today he was wearing a fancy green turban and a gold cape!

"Wow," Nancy said. "Toby looks like someone out of the story 'Aladdin.'"

"So does that tent," Bess said. "But what's it doing on the playground?"

"I'll bet Toby is putting on some kind of play," George said. "Let's ask him."

As the girls walked closer Nancy saw a sign

pinned to the tent: HOT CHOCOLATE WITH MARSH-MALLOWS. $1.00.

"Are we lucky or what?" George said.

"Hi, Toby," Nancy said. "Can we have some—"

"Stop!" Toby said. He held up his hand like a school crossing guard. "You must wait your turn!"

The flap of the tent swung open. A girl burst out with a big smile. "Yes!" She pumped her fist.

"I'm going to be an astronaut when I grow up! I'm going to the moon! The moon!"

Nancy, Bess, and George traded puzzled looks.

What was going on in there?

Toby folded his arms across his chest. "Madame Coco Chocolata will see you now!" he announced in a deep voice.

"Madame Chocolata?" George whispered.

"Who is Madame Chocolata?" Bess whispered back.

Nancy stared at the tent. This was way too weird!

"I don't have a clue," Nancy said. She took a step toward the tent. "But there's only one way to find out!"

CHAPTER TWO

Snow Problem!

"Close the flap!" a voice cried. "It's freezing out there!"

The girls stooped to get into the tent. Nancy smiled when she saw their classmate Deirdre Shannon inside. Deirdre was sitting cross-legged on a blanket. She wore a gold turban, hoop earrings, and beaded necklaces over her down jacket. On the blanket was a thermos, a stack of paper cups, and a bag of mini-marshmallows.

"Hi, Deirdre!" Nancy said.

"What's up?" George asked. "Halloween was months ago."

"I am not this Deirdre you speak of," Deirdre

said. "I am Madame Coco Chocolata—teller of fortunes!"

"Fortunes?" Nancy, Bess, and George said together.

Deirdre's turban almost fell off as she nodded her head. "Some fortune-tellers read palms. Others read tea leaves," she explained. "But I, Madame Chocolata, read the marshmallows in hot chocolate!"

"Huh?" George said.

Deirdre picked up the thermos and smiled. "For just one dollar you get a steaming cup of cocoa," she said, "and your life's destiny."

Nancy glanced sideways at her friends. Deirdre Shannon always got whatever she wanted— which probably explained the fancy tent. But she was usually busy working on her website, Dishing with Deirdre.

"Whoever heard of reading marshmallows?" Bess whispered.

"She's got hot chocolate," George whispered. "Who cares what she does with it?"

"Thanks, Deirdre," Nancy said. "We'll each have a cup . . . and our fortunes!"

"And so you shall!" Deirdre said. As she poured hot chocolate into three cups, Nancy chatted about Sherlock.

"You should go and see him, Deirdre," Nancy said. "He's the best snowman ever!"

"Really? What does he look like?" Deirdre asked.

"You're the fortune-teller." Bess giggled. "You tell us!"

Nancy jabbed Bess with her elbow. Deirdre was taking this game very seriously!

"Sherlock has a blue scarf and a broccoli nose," Nancy said. "And he's right near the water fountain."

"Which isn't really a water fountain today because the water's frozen," George added.

Deirdre lined the white cups in a row. "Quick!" she said. "I must read your fortunes before my trance breaks. And before the mini-marshmallows melt."

The girls sat cross-legged in front of Deirdre. "Madame Chocolata will read Nancy's fortune first," Deirdre said. She stared into a cup without blinking. "I see a pizza in your future. A large pizza with extra cheese. Madame Chocolata predicts pizza for dinner tonight!"

"If you say so," Nancy said. "But my dad only orders pizza on Saturday nights—"

"Next!" Deirdre said a little too loudly.

"That's me," George said. "What do you see in my hot chocolate? Am I going to get that neat computerized watch I want?"

Nancy smiled. George loved computers more than anything. She even had a computerized toothbrush!

"I see a snowman," Deirdre said slowly. She stared into the cup. "Near the water fountain."

"Ye-ah! We just told you that," George said.

"Wait!" Deirdre said. She leaned over as she stared deeply into George's cup. "The snowman is taking a long, long journey. He is walking . . . walking . . ."

George laughed and said, "Snowmen can't walk—"

"Next!" Deirdre cut in.

"Bess, that's you," Nancy said.

"This is too silly," Bess said, shaking her head. "I don't want to play. I just want a cup of hot chocolate with marshmallows, please."

Deirdre narrowed her eyes at Bess. She waved her hands over the last cup of hot chocolate and said, "I see a big ice show! I see someone falling on the ice! And lots of people laughing and saying, 'What a klutz! What a klutz!'"

"What?" Bess gasped. "You mean I'm going to fall in the Ice Spectacular? With Svetlana and Alexi Dubonov?"

"It's in the marshmallows," Deirdre said with a shrug. "That will be three dollars, please. Have a nice day."

The girls dropped their dollar bills into a basket. They sipped their hot chocolate as they left the tent.

"Nancy, George!" Bess cried. "What if Deirdre really can see the future? She already knew I was in the show!"

"Who *doesn't* know?" George said. She licked a marshmallow from her upper lip. "You told practically the whole school. And the world!"

"Deirdre is just doing this for fun," Nancy

said. "Come on. I want to show you something."

The girls finished their hot chocolate as they made their way over to Sherlock. Nancy pointed to their snowman and smiled.

"See?" Nancy said. "Sherlock didn't take a long journey like Deirdre said. He's still where we left him."

Bess smiled and said, "You're right. I guess it was kind of silly."

"If anyone is a klutz, it's me!" Nancy said. She pointed to a stain on her scarf. "See? I already dripped hot chocolate all over myself!"

The girls watched as a bird landed on the broccoli nose. They giggled as he began pecking at it.

"At least somebody likes broccoli!" George said. "Let's go home now, before my toes turn into toesicles!"

Nancy, Bess, and George left the park. They all had the same rules. They could walk anywhere as long as it was no more than five blocks from their houses. And as long as they were together.

"Let's come back to the park tomorrow," George said. "We can make snow angels and have a snowball fight."

"Maybe we can build a snow*woman*!" Nancy said.

"Okay," Bess said with a groan. "But from now on, let's bring our own hot chocolate!"

"Can people read fortunes, Daddy?" Nancy asked at the dinner table that night.

Mr. Drew shrugged as he poured dressing over his salad. He was a lawyer and great at figuring things out. "Some people say they do," he said. "They read palms. Or tea leaves. Or—"

"Marshmallows?" Nancy said.

"Did you say marshmallows?" Mr. Drew asked.

"Deirdre says she can read the marshmallows in hot chocolate," Nancy explained. "But it didn't work. She said we'd have pizza tonight—"

"And we're having vegetable lasagna!" Hannah

said as she carried a casserole dish into the dining room.

Hannah Gruen was the Drews' housekeeper. Hannah had been taking very good care of Nancy since Nancy was three years old. That's when Nancy's mother had died. Hannah brushed Nancy's reddish-blond hair every morning until it shined. She made the best tuna sandwiches with tomatoes. And Hannah always smelled like sugar cookies—even when she wasn't baking!

"Yummy!" Nancy said. She took a whiff of the hot steaming lasagna. "Who needs pizza when we can have this?"

Just then the doorbell rang.

"Who could that be at dinnertime?" Mr. Drew asked.

Nancy glanced at the clock in the dining room. It was six o'clock. Sharp.

Mr. Drew left the room to answer the door. When he came back he was holding a big flat box. "Did anyone order this?" he asked.

Nancy stared at the box. There was only one thing that came in a box like that!

"Pizza?" Nancy gasped. "No way!"

"Maybe Hannah ordered the pizza," George said. "To go with the lasagna!"

It was Wednesday morning. The girls were walking through the main gate of the park. It was so cold they wore layers of fleece shirts under their parkas.

"Hannah said she didn't," Nancy said. "She even called Pizza Paradise. They said someone ordered the pie at five thirty but didn't leave a name."

"Omigosh!" Bess gasped. "Madame Chocolata

said you'd have pizza for dinner and she was right!"

Nancy smiled as she shook her head. "Daddy and I figured it out," she said. "Deirdre probably ordered the pizza herself to make it look like her fortune came true."

"But I saw Deirdre at the mall yesterday," George said. "She was trying on shoes with her mother. And it was exactly five thirty."

"How do you know it was exactly five thirty?" Nancy asked.

George pulled up her sleeve to show a hi-tech silver watch. "Because I got the computerized watch I wanted," she said excitedly. "I couldn't stop looking at it!"

Nancy's heart sank. She'd thought she had the whole thing figured out, but she didn't.

"If Deirdre was trying on shoes at five thirty," she said, "then she couldn't have ordered the pizza."

Bess stopped walking. Her eyes flashed with fear.

"If Deirdre was right about the pizza then she'll be right about me," Bess said. "I'm going to fall on the ice in front of hundreds of people!"

"Right," Nancy chuckled. "And our snowman will take a long journey too!"

"As if that's going to happen!" George laughed.

Bess finally smiled too. "You're right," she said. "The only snowman who can walk is Frosty!"

The girls began singing "Frosty the Snowman." Their singing stopped when they reached the water fountain.

Nancy, Bess, and George looked around. Something was missing.

"Um . . . Bess, George?" Nancy said. "Where's Sherlock?"

CHAPTER THREE

Snowball Fright

"Are we sure this is the right spot?" Bess asked.

"Totally," Nancy said.

The three friends stared at the empty spot in the snow—the spot where Sherlock had been standing just yesterday.

"Maybe he melted," Nancy said.

"He couldn't have melted," George said. "The temperature is still below freezing. And all the other snowmen from yesterday are still around."

"Then what happened to Sherlock?" Bess asked. "Did he take a walk? Just like Deirdre said he would?"

Nancy walked to the spot where Sherlock

had stood. She patted the snow on the ground. "Someone probably knocked him down," she said. "That's all."

"Then where is Sherlock's scarf?" George asked. "And his broccoli nose? And my dad's old boots?"

"I don't know," Nancy admitted. She saw a big footprint in the snow. Looking up she saw a whole trail of footprints leading away from the site.

"Look," Nancy said. "Whoever knocked down Sherlock left footprints."

George tilted her head as she studied a print. "The soles had a diamond design—just like my dad's old boots," she said. "The boots we put on Sherlock."

"Then Sherlock did walk away!" Bess gasped. "Just like Deirdre said he would."

Nancy shook her head. She didn't believe for a minute that Deirdre was a fortune-teller. There had to be a reason that Sherlock wasn't there!

"Hey, guys!" a voice called out.

Nancy turned. Their friends Marcy Rubin and Trina Vanderhoof were walking over. Trina's thick furry boots made loud clomping sounds in the snow. Marcy wore blue rubber boots with a pretty white snowflake design.

"Guess where we're going?" Marcy asked.

"To the beach!" George joked. "To swim with the polar bears and penguins!"

"Very funny," Trina said with a smirk. "We're going to see Madame Chocolata!"

Oh, no, Nancy thought. *Not them too!*

"Trina and I saw Madame Chocolata yesterday," Marcy said.

"She told me I'd get a bright and shiny surprise."

"What did that mean?" Nancy asked.

"Ta-daa!" Marcy sang. She held up her wrist to show a bracelet with glittery pink beads. "This was in my mailbox this morning. Isn't it awesome?"

"Totally," Bess muttered.

"Madame Chocolata said I'd get a new basketball," Trina chimed in. "And this morning I found a basketball in my front yard! How cool is that?"

"Way cool," Bess muttered again.

"Who needs a magic eight ball when you have Madame Chocolata?" Marcy said.

"Her hot chocolate is pretty good too," Trina said. "Come on, Marcy. Let's see what's in the marshmallows today!"

"Maybe I'll get earrings to match my bracelet!" Marcy said excitedly.

Nancy, Bess, and George were silent as their friends walked toward the playground.

"I have to go to the ice-skating rink now," Bess said in a small voice.

"To practice?" George asked.

"No," Bess said. "To *quit*!"

Nancy felt bad for Bess. Skating with Alexi and Svetlana was her dream—Nancy couldn't let Deirdre spoil it!

"Deirdre is not a fortune-teller," Nancy said with a firm voice. "And the Clue Crew is going to prove it!"

"How are we going to prove it?" Bess asked.

"By finding out what *really* happened to Sherlock, that's how," Nancy said with a smile.

"Another mystery!" George cheered. She pumped her fist in the air. "Bring it on!"

Nancy looked at Bess. She didn't seem excited. Just worried. "Bess?" she asked slowly. "We're not the Clue Crew without you too."

Bess giggled at the rhyme. "Okay. I'm in," she said.

"Cool!" Nancy said. "The Clue Crew is on the case!"

The girls were about to high-five when—*whap*! A snowball hit a nearby tree. As it exploded, sticky yellow stuff dripped down the trunk!

"Ewww!" Bess said. "What is that?"

"It looks like egg," Nancy said, scrunching up her nose. "I think that snowball had a raw egg inside."

"Look out!" George shouted.

Another snowball whizzed over Nancy's head. It burst on the ground, splattering egg all over the snow. The girls ducked as more eggy snowballs flew by fast and furiously.

"It's an attack!" Bess cried.

Nancy tried to see through the whirl of snow and eggs. The egg-balls seemed to be coming from behind a snow-covered bench!

George was about to make her own snowball when—*thwack*! One exploded on the sleeve of her parka!

"Gross!" George said. She watched as sticky egg yolk dripped down her sleeve. "I am never eating scrambled eggs again!"

The icky snowballs finally stopped. The girls
waited until they were sure the coast was clear.
Then they walked slowly and carefully to the
bench.

Nancy peeked behind it. A half-empty carton of eggs lay on the ground. Next to the box were letters carved into the snow.

"It looks like a message!" Nancy said.

The girls hurried around the bench. Nancy read the message out loud. It said:

"Gotcha! The Snowman!"

CHAPTER FOUR

Cold Case

"A snowman did this?" Bess cried. "Maybe it was Sherlock!"

"How could Sherlock be so mean?" George asked. "We gave him a smile!"

"But a broccoli nose!" Bess added. "No wonder he wants to get even with us."

"Oh, so now it's my fault?" George demanded.

"You guys, you guys!" Nancy said. "It might not be a *real* snowman!"

"Then who is it?" George asked.

"I don't know," Nancy said. "But we'll find out."

"I thought we were going to look for Sherlock!" Bess said.

"The pest who threw those eggs could have knocked down Sherlock too," Nancy explained. "So let's start looking for clues."

The girls squatted down to study the message. Nancy found some woolly green threads inside the letters.

"The person who wrote the message must have been wearing something green," Nancy said. She carefully picked up two threads. Then she dropped them into one of the plastic bags she always carried around "in case of a case."

Bess pointed to the message.

"Look at the letter *S*," she said. "It's written in a curly way. Like a snake."

George found footprints leading away from the message. They were smaller than the ones near Sherlock. And instead of a diamond design, they had a starry design on the soles.

Nancy and George wanted to look for more clues. But Bess had other plans. She had to practice for the ice show that afternoon.

"Can we watch?" George asked excitedly. "I'd love to see Alexi and Svetlana Dubonov skate!"

"And Bess Marvin!" Nancy added quickly.

The girls hooked arms and walked through the snow. On the way out of the park they saw Marcy's little sister Cassidy. The six-year-old was lying on her back making snow angels. As she waved her arms up and down, she sang at the top of her lungs: "I'm getting a puppy! A cute little puppy!"

Nancy, Bess, and George stood over Cassidy.

"Did your parents say you can have a puppy?" Nancy asked.

"No, silly!" Cassidy said. "Madame Chocolata said I'd get one."

Nancy groaned under her breath. Madame

Chocolata! Madame Chocolata! Madame Chocolata!

"Not everyone believes in Madame Chocolata, you know," Nancy said as they kept walking.

"Oh, yeah?" George said. She pointed to a long line of kids outside Deirdre's tent. They were all chanting, "We want Madame Chocolata! We want Madame Chocolata!"

Nancy stared at the crowd. Then she shrugged her shoulders and said, "So they want hot chocolate. Big deal."

Nancy and George got permission to watch Bess practice. An hour later Mrs. Marvin drove the girls to the ice-skating rink in her red van. As Mrs. Marvin parked on River Street, Nancy glanced out the window. She saw Toby Leo standing in front of the Toys 4 You store. His nose was pressed against the glass window as he gazed at the new sleds.

Maybe Madame Chocolata told him he'd get a new sled, Nancy thought glumly.

Inside the rink Nancy and George sat on

the bottom bleacher. They cheered for Bess as she skated out on the ice. She wasn't wearing her costume yet—just a pair of pink sweats. Svetlana and Alexi skated out to meet Bess. They were wearing matching black and silver bodysuits. Still skating, Alexi lifted Svetlana way over his head!

"There they are," Nancy whispered.

"They are so awesome!" George said.

Alexi and Svetlana skated over to Bess.

"Today we practice as if we're in the show!" Svetlana announced with a Russian accent.

"Hit music!" Alexi called out.

The song "Winter Wonderland" blared through the loudspeakers. Svetlana, Bess, and Alexi held hands as they glided across the ice.

"I can't believe Bess is skating with Svetlana and Alexi Dubonov!" George whispered.

Nancy turned to George and said, "And she hasn't fallen once!"

"Whoooaaaa!"

Nancy turned her head just in time to see

Bess sliding across the ice on her bottom!

"Oh, noooo!" Nancy cried.

"Stop music! Stop music!" Alexi shouted.

Bess slid to a stop but didn't stand up. She just sat on the ice with her head bowed.

"Don't worry, Bess," Svetlana said.

"Even we fall sometimes!" Alexi said. He pointed to his knee. "See? Hole in tights!"

Bess forced a little smile. She let Svetlana and Alexi help her to her feet.

Mrs. Marvin sat on the bleacher behind Nancy and George. "Oh, dear," she said. "Bess must be a bit nervous."

George leaned over to Nancy. "Or she's thinking about what Madame Chocolata told her," she whispered.

Nancy nodded sadly.

The ice show was in three days. If they were going to find out what happened to Sherlock, they would have to find out *fast*!

CHAPTER FIVE

Pranks a Lot!

"I'm such a loser," Bess said. "Maybe I should get training wheels for my skates! Or maybe Alexi and Svetlana should carry me onto the ice instead. Like a big baby!"

It was Thursday morning. The park was still covered with snow as the girls made their way through the main gate.

"You're not a loser or a baby, Bess," Nancy said. "You were just nervous."

"Sure!" George said. "I'd be nervous too if I had to skate with stars like Svetlana and Alexi. And if hundreds of people were watching me."

"Gee, thanks," Bess groaned. "I feel much better now!"

"Make way for the great Madame Chocolata!" a voice declared.

Nancy turned and saw Toby walking into the park. He was dragging the rolled-up purple and gold tent. Walking a few steps behind him was Deirdre. They were both dressed in their turbans and capes.

"There she is," George whispered. "The Marshmallow Medium!"

Nancy saw a white picnic cooler in Deirdre's hand, probably filled with hot chocolate, cups, and marshmallows.

Nancy was about to say hi when two kids ran over.

"It's her! It's Madame Chocolata!" a girl said.

"Madame Chocolata—you rock!" said a boy.

"Thank you, thank you," Deirdre said. She held up her hand. "But no autographs, please!"

As the kids walked away, Deirdre turned to Nancy, Bess, and George. Her eyes flashed with excitement.

"Do you believe it? Almost all of my fortunes

are coming true!" Deirdre squealed. "And I only became Madame Chocolata because I wanted kids to read my website. Now I'm totally famous—like a rock star!"

Give me a break, Nancy thought. She hoped Bess and George wouldn't tell Deirdre about their missing snowman. It would just give her another reason to brag!

"What do you think of Madame Chocolata fortune cookies?" Deirdre asked. "They would be chocolate-flavored fortune cookies, of course—"

"Whoa!" Toby shouted. "Check it out!"

Nancy looked to see where Toby was pointing. A few feet away were some bushes wrapped with white toilet paper. The kids walked over to the bushes to check them out.

"It looks like some kind of prank," George said.

A note was stuck to a branch. It was written in green ink. Nancy pulled it off and read it to herself. She blinked and read it again to make sure it was right.

"Nancy! What does it say?" Bess asked.

"It says," Nancy said slowly, "'That's a wrap! The Snowman.'"

"The Snowman again!" Bess gasped.

"What Snowman?" Deirdre asked.

"Um," Nancy said. "Er . . ."

Nancy wanted to change the subject, so she was happy to see their friends Kendra Jackson and Nadine Nardo walking by. But Kendra and Nadine looked sad as they pulled sleds covered with sticky green Silly String.

"Why did you squirt Silly String all over your sleds?" Deirdre asked. "Is it a cool new look?"

"We didn't do it," Kendra grumbled.

"Kendra and I left our sleds by a tree while we made snow angels," Nadine explained. "When we came back for our sleds they looked like this!"

"Do you know who did it?" Nancy asked.

Kendra shrugged and said, "Some weird message was written in the snow with pebbles. It said, 'The Snowman Was Here.'"

"No way!" George exclaimed. "The Snowman struck again!"

"And I'll bet he's Sherlock!" Bess said.

"Sherlock?" Deirdre asked. "You mean that snowman you built yesterday?"

Nancy raised her eyebrow at Bess as if to say, "Don't tell her." But Bess was already babbling on. . . .

"Our snowman did take a journey just like you said, Madame Chocolata," Bess said. "And now he's making trouble in the park!"

"Cool!" Deirdre exclaimed.

"What's so cool about that?" Nancy asked.

"It means another one of my fortunes came

true!" Deirdre said. "The great Madame Chocolata scores again!"

"Yeah," Toby said. He sagged from the weight of the tent. "Scores again."

Deirdre and Toby left to set up the tent. Nadine and Kendra turned to the girls with angry eyes.

"Who did you build anyway?" Nadine asked. "Frosty's evil twin?"

"You built him," Kendra said. "Now you *stop* him."

Kendra and Nadine huffed away with their sleds.

"Wow," George said. "We didn't build a snowman. We created a Frankenstein."

Nancy didn't get it. How could both her friends believe their snowman was alive? How could they believe in Madame Chocolata?

"Come on, Clue Crew," Nancy said. "Let's find out who's *really* making all this trouble. And I'll bet it's not Sherlock!"

The girls went back to work. They found more green threads on the bushes. As Bess and

George picked them up, Nancy gazed thought-fully in the distance.

This really is a mystery, Nancy thought. *Who could the Snowman be?*

Suddenly something big and white dashed out from behind a tree. A bright blue scarf fluttered from its neck as it darted from tree to tree.

"Yikes!" Nancy gasped.

"Nancy—are you okay?" Bess asked.

"Yeah," George said. "You look like you just saw a ghost!"

ChaPTeR Six

Snowman or No-man?

Nancy gulped.

She wasn't sure *what* she saw. So she decided to keep the snowman part to herself.

"I think I saw . . . a giant white squirrel," Nancy blurted. "Yeah, that's it."

Bess and George exchanged looks.

"A giant white squirrel?" Bess repeated.

"Was he carrying a giant nut?" George chuckled.

Nancy shook her head and smiled. "I think my eyes played a trick on me," she said. "Let's go to our detective headquarters and sort out our clues."

"Good idea," Bess said. "It's so cold my face feels like it fell asleep!"

As they walked away, Nancy glanced over her shoulder at the trees. She didn't see anything big, white, and blue this time.

All this talk about walking snowmen, Nancy thought. *No wonder I imagined it!*

Bess stopped at a garbage can. It was filled with bright pink papers.

"Hey!" Bess said, looking inside. "These are for the Ice Spectacular Show. But what are they doing in a garbage can?"

"Come on, Bess," George said, tugging her cousin's arm. "We may be detectives, but we can't figure everything out."

Nancy, Bess, and George were happy

to reach the toasty-warm Drew house. When Hannah saw the shivering girls she poured three bowls of steaming-hot tomato soup.

"What did you girls do in the park today?" Hannah asked. "Build a snowman?"

Nancy, Bess, and George sat around the kitchen table eating their soup.

"We built a snowman two days ago," Nancy said.

"Now we're trying to find him," George said.

"Find him?" Hannah said. "Do you think he melted?"

"No," Nancy, Bess, and George said together.

"Well, then," Hannah chuckled. "He couldn't have just up and walked away!"

The girls exchanged looks around the table.

"Um," Nancy said slowly. "May we have some crackers, please?"

After lunch the girls hurried up to Nancy's room. George sat at Nancy's computer to start a new detective file. She named it "What Happened to Sherlock?" Nancy and Bess carefully placed the green threads and the note into the clue drawer in Nancy's desk.

"I still don't get it," Bess said. "If somebody knocked down Sherlock, what happened to his things? Like his scarf, his boots, the dog kibbles, and the broccoli nose?"

"The guilty person probably took them," Nancy decided. "Or hid them somewhere."

"Poor Sherlock," George said, sighing as she typed. "Such an awesome snowman—totally wiped out!"

Wiped out? Wipeout!

"Remember the kid on the snowboard?" Nancy asked. "He yelled 'wipeout' before he almost knocked down Sherlock."

"But he *didn't* knock him down," Bess said.

"He could have come back to finish the job!" Nancy said. "If only we knew his name so we could find him."

"Maybe he goes to our school," George said. "He looked like he could have been in fourth grade."

Nancy didn't know many kids in fourth grade. But she did know her good friend Ned Nickerson!

"I'll ask Ned!" Nancy said. "He knows everybody!"

George stood up so Nancy could sit down at the computer. Nancy clicked the mouse and went online. As she scrolled down her buddy list she saw Ned's screen name. He was online too!

Bess and George peered over Nancy's shoulder as she sent Ned an instant message: "Hi Ned. Do U know a fourth grader who snowboards in the park?"

The girls waited for Ned's answer. After a few seconds they heard a chime. Ned's message popped up on the screen:

"Bradley Sorensen. He's bad news!"

"Bad news? Sounds like our man!" George said.

Nancy IM'd Ned again: "How can I find him?"

"Send him an IM," Ned sent back. "His screen name is easy 2 remember."

"What is it?" Nancy typed. She waited for Ned's message. When it popped up the girls stared at the screen. Bradley's screen name was—

"The Snowman!" Nancy gasped.

ChAPTER SEVEN

Chill on the Hill

"That's the name we found at the scenes of the crimes," George exclaimed. "Bradley's got to be guilty!"

"Go ahead, Nancy!" Bess said. She pointed to the keyboard. "Send Bradley an instant message!"

Nancy thanked Ned and signed off. "I think I'd rather question Bradley face to face first," she said. "If we can find him again."

"We can look for Bradley in the park," George said.

Nancy thought about Bradley's fancy moves on his snowboard. "Or we can look for him somewhere else," she said.

"Where?" Bess and George asked together.

"Nightmare Hill!" Nancy said with a grin.

"Whoa!" George cried. "That's the steepest hill in River Heights!"

"You have to be superbrave to go down Nightmare Hill," Bess said. "Or supercrazy!"

Nancy thought of Bradley and said, "Exactly!"

Nightmare Hill was five blocks away. The girls had permission to walk there together. As they stood on the hilltop they saw a few extreme sledders and snowboarders. But not Bradley.

"I guess even Bradley's not crazy enough to go down Nightmare Hill." Nancy sighed.

They were about to walk away when someone yelled, "King of the hill! I'm king of the hill! Woo-hooooo!"

Nancy whipped around. Zipping down the hill on his snowboard was Bradley Sorensen. He was wearing black ski goggles, a blue parka, and matching pants. Suddenly Nancy noticed something else. . . .

"Look at Bradley's gloves!" Nancy said. "They're

green—the same color as those woolly threads we found!"

"I told you he was guilty!" George said.

"Not yet," Nancy said. "There's one more thing I want to find out."

Bradley began climbing back up the hill.

"Bradley Sorensen!" Nancy called. "I can't believe it! Can I have your autograph? Can I? Can I?"

"Huh?" George said.

"Nancy . . . yuck," Bess whispered.

Bradley looked surprised too. "My what?" he asked.

"Your autograph!" Nancy said. "You're going to be a famous Olympic snowboarder someday. So I want to be the first fan to get your autograph!"

"I think I'm going to barf," George muttered.

Bradley grinned. He reached into his pocket and pulled out an empty candy bar wrapper. Then he pulled out a pen. Nancy watched as Bradley scribbled his name on the wrapper.

"Here," Bradley said. He held out the wrapper.

"But next time I charge five bucks!"

Nancy snatched the wrapper. She looked at the autograph and shouted—

"Just as I thought. Green ink!"

Bess jabbed the autograph.

"And look!" she said. "The letter *S* is curly. The same as the messages!"

"What are you girlies talking about?" Bradley cried.

"You're the one who did all those mean pranks in the park," Nancy said. "You're the Snowman!"

Bradley narrowed his eyes at the girls. Then he slipped his feet into his snowboard and said, "Oh, yeah? Catch me if you can!"

The girls watched as Bradley pushed down the hill.

"Oh, great," George said. "He's getting away!"

Bess glanced around. She ran over to a big sheet of cardboard and dragged it over.

"What's that?" Nancy asked.

"An instant sled," Bess said. "Hop on!"

"But this is Nightmare Hill!" George cried.

They sat in a row on the cardboard. Then they leaned forward and pushed it down the hill!

"Whoaaaaaaaa!" the girls shouted.

Nancy gritted her teeth as they sped after Bradley. It was like being on the bumpiest, scariest roller-coaster ride!

"King of the hill!" Bradley shouted as he gained speed. "King of the—aaaaaaah!"

Bradley's snowboard flipped over. He flew through the air and landed right in a snowbank.

The cardboard sled stopped at the bottom of the hill. The girls jumped off and ran to Bradley. He was standing up covered with snow.

"Now you're king of the *spill*!" George laughed.

"Why did you do it, Bradley?" Nancy asked. "Why did you do all those pranks?"

"I don't know what you're talking about!" Bradley growled.

Bradley dusted himself off. Suddenly Nancy spotted something stuck to his sleeve. It looked like a strand of green Silly String!

"I think you *do* know what I'm talking about," Nancy said. She plucked the string from his sleeve and smiled.

Bradley stared at the string and sighed.

"Okay, so I squirted a bunch of sleds," he said. "And papered some bushes. And threw some eggs. Big deal!"

"You forgot something," George said. "You knocked down our snowman too."

"No way!" Bradley said. "That I didn't do!"

"You didn't?" Nancy asked.

"Nah!" Bradley said. "I stopped knocking down snowmen in second grade!"

Bradley picked up his board. Then he stomped his way up the hill.

"How do we know he's telling the truth?" Bess asked.

George pointed to one of Bradley's footprints.

"His boots have that starry design on the sole," George said. "Just like the footprints near the pranks."

"But not like the ones near Sherlock," Bess said.

"I don't think Bradley knocked down Sherlock," Nancy said. "And he won't make any more trouble either now that we know who the Snowman is."

"But we still don't know what happened to Sherlock," George said.

Nancy, Bess, and George chatted as they walked away from the hill. The friends still couldn't believe they had sledded down the highest hill in River Heights!

"And I built a sled!" Bess said proudly. "Well . . . sort of!"

The girls headed back to the Drew house. Nancy's puppy Chocolate Chip was tethered to a tree in the front yard. The chain fastened to Chip's collar was long enough for her to romp around in the snow.

Chip buried her little brown face in the snow. When she pulled it out, it was completely white!

"Chip loves the snow!" Nancy said.

"I can see that!" George laughed.

Inside the house the girls sat around the

kitchen table drinking Hannah's yummy hot chocolate. They forgot all about the case as they giggled and licked chocolate mustaches from their lips. As they sipped their last drops Hannah held out Chip's leash.

"Now that you've had some hot chocolate," Hannah said, "how about walking Chocolate Chip?"

Nancy, Bess, and George bundled up again and went outside. Chip's chain was still attached to the tree. But Chip was gone!

Nancy's heart beat faster and faster. "B-Bess, George!" she stammered. "Somebody took my dog!"

CHAPTER EIGHT

Chip, Chip, Hooray!

Nancy was about to shout for Hannah when she heard a bark. She ran onto the sidewalk and looked down the street. A boy was carrying Chip away!

"It looks like Toby Leo!" Nancy said.

"What's he doing with Chip?" Bess asked.

Chip's ears flopped up and down as Toby hurried down the block. "Toby—stop!" Nancy shouted.

Toby looked over his shoulder. His mouth dropped open when he saw the girls. Chip barked. As she jumped out of Toby's arms she dragged the scarf off his neck.

"Sorry, Nancy!" Toby called as he ran away. "I didn't mean it! Honest!"

The girls raced over to Chip. Nancy scooped
her up and held her tight. She attached Chip's
leash to her puppy's collar.

"Why would Toby take Chip?" Nancy asked.

"Maybe he wanted a puppy," Bess said with a
shrug. "Everybody wants a cute little puppy."

Nancy thought of Cassidy making snow angels and singing about a puppy. That's when it began to click.

"Didn't Madame Chocolata tell Cassidy she would get a puppy?" Nancy asked.

"Yeah, so?" George said.

"Maybe Toby took Chip to give to Cassidy!" Nancy said. "So it would look like Deirdre's fortune came true!"

"Maybe Toby is making *all* of Madame Chocolata's fortunes come true!" George said. "Like Marcy's bracelet. And Trina's basketball—"

"And Sherlock!" Bess gasped.

Nancy picked up the scarf. It had a tiny hole at the end, just like the one she had wrapped around Sherlock.

"Toby lives right around the corner," Nancy said. She tied the scarf around her own neck. "Let's see what we can find out."

The Clue Crew walked Chip around the corner to the Leo house. George rang the doorbell. When no one answered they headed around the house to the backyard. There was a swing set and a snow-covered picnic table.

But no Toby.

Just then Chip tugged at her leash. The little puppy pulled Nancy in the direction of a tree.

"What is it, girl?" Nancy asked.

"Maybe she has to go again," George said.

But when Chip stopped at the tree she started digging. She dug and dug until she reached something in the snow. Nancy could see they were little round dog kibbles.

"Bess, George, look!" Nancy said. "Those are the same kind of kibbles we used for Sherlock's nose and mouth!"

"What else is down there?" George asked.

While Chip munched on the kibbles, the girls brushed away more snow. Buried underneath was a pair of old rubber boots.

"My dad's boots!" George exclaimed.

Nancy picked one up. It felt heavy. She tipped it over and a stalk of broccoli and earmuffs spilled out!

"Those are the earmuffs I made for Sherlock!"
Bess cried. "And that's his broccoli nose!"

Nancy scratched Chip behind her ears. "Good
girl, Chip!" she said. "You found some awesome
clues. And I think we found the person who
knocked down Sherlock!"

Nancy hurried to bring Chip home. Then
the Clue Crew marched straight to the park.

They walked past a long line of kids in front of Madame Chocolata's tent.

"Hey! Wait your turn!" a boy shouted out.

"Quit jumping the line!" a girl said.

"Um—we're delivering marshmallows," George said quickly. "Can't tell fortunes without marsh-mallows!"

The girls slipped inside the tent. Deirdre and Toby were sitting on the blanket counting dollar bills.

"Fifteen, sixteen," Toby counted. "Seventeen—"

"Toby Leo!" Nancy snapped.

"Wha!" Toby cried. The dollars flew out of his hands as he jumped up. "Nancy! I-I g-gave you back your dog!"

"What's up?" Deirdre asked. "I mean—what

can Madame Chocolata tell you today?"

"How about telling us if Toby knocked down our snowman," Nancy said.

"Tell us, Toby," George said. "Or we'll tell your parents that you took Nancy's dog right out of her yard!"

"I told you I didn't mean to take the puppy!" Toby said. "It was temporary insanity! Temporary insanity!"

"Dog? Snowman?" Deirdre said. "What's going on?"

Toby hung his head. "Okay, okay," he said. "I've been listening in on your fortunes, Deirdre. And I've been making them come true."

"What?" Deirdre gasped.

"I knocked down their snowman," Toby went on.

"I even put on his boots and walked out of the park—so it would look like his footsteps!"

"And you buried the boots in your yard," Nancy said. "Along with the kibbles, the earmuffs, the broccoli nose—"

"But I kept the scarf!" Toby cut in. He pointed to the scarf around Nancy's neck. "Blue is my favorite color!"

"Why did you do it, Toby?" Bess asked.

"So Madame Chocolata would have lots of customers," Toby explained. "We were split-ting the money even-steven. The more money I got, the more I'd have to buy that new sled I wanted."

Nancy got it. No wonder Toby was staring into the toy store window yesterday.

"But I had to use all my money to buy stuff like pizzas and plastic bracelets," Toby said with a frown. "I even gave Trina Vanderhoof one of my own basketballs because I couldn't afford to buy a new one."

Deirdre glared at Toby long and hard.

"All this time I thought my fortunes were coming true!" she said between gritted teeth. "I was going to have my own fortune cookies! A new website! I was even going to write a best-selling book called *Mystic Marshmallows!*"

"Sorry, Deirdre," Toby said. "Once I started I couldn't quit. But I'll quit now. I promise!"

Deirdre reached up and pulled off her turban. "Well, if I can't tell fortunes, then I quit too!" she declared.

"What?" Nancy, Bess, and George said together.

"These hoop earrings pinch and this stupid tent is freezing," Deirdre groaned. "And if I have to stare at one more marshmallow I'll flip!"

"So you're not Madame Chocolata anymore?" Nancy asked.

"I am so over it!" Deirdre said. She turned to Bess. "I'm sorry I said you'd fall on the ice. I was just mad you called me silly."

"And I'm sorry I called you silly," Bess said.

Nancy was so happy she could do cartwheels. The Clue Crew solved the case. And Bess and Deirdre made up!

Just then the kids outside the tent began to shout.

"We want Madame Chocolata! We want

Madame Chocolata! We want Madame Choco-lata!"

"Uh-oh," Nancy said. "How are you going to tell all those kids that you quit?"

"Oh, *I'm* not telling them," Deirdre said. She crossed her arms and turned to Toby.

"Me?" Toby squeaked.

Nancy, Bess, and George slipped out of the tent past the crowd.

"Did you hear that?" Bess said happily. "Deirdre made up the fortune that I'd fall in the show!"

"And Toby confessed to knocking down Sher-lock!" Nancy said. "So we solved the case!"

They were about to high-five when Nancy saw something big and white flit by in the distance. This time Bess and George saw it too.

"Did you see that?" Bess gasped. "It looked like a walking snowman!"

"He's back," Nancy said slowly.

"Back?" George said. "You mean you saw him once before?"

Nancy explained how she had seen a figure that looked like a snowman. But she hadn't said anything because she wasn't sure if she saw it or not.

The girls walked carefully to where they had seen the figure, but all they could see were his footprints. They weren't like the footprints the boots had made, though. They were huge deep holes in the snow.

Nancy, Bess, and George were silent as they stared at the strange footprints.

"This case is not closed," Nancy said. "Not until we find out who that was."

"Or *what* it was," Bess said with a shiver.

That night Nancy sat in the den watching TV. She wasn't really paying attention, though. She was too busy wondering about the mysterious figure they had seen in the park that day.

It looked like a snowman, Nancy thought. *But was it a snowman?*

Nancy clicked the remote to surf the channels. She stopped when she saw a news reporter standing in front of the River Heights Museum of Natural History. It was Nancy's favorite museum. It even had dinosaur bones inside!

"There have been many sightings of the Yeti," the reporter said. "Also known as the Abominable Snowman."

Nancy sat up straight.

Did she say "snowman"?

Chapter Nine

Heads Up!

Nancy turned up the sound.

"A special exhibit on the Abominable Snowman opened at the museum today," the reporter was saying. "So come in and enjoy rare pictures of the famous walking snowman!"

"Walking snowman?" Nancy gasped. "Omigosh!"

Nancy raced to find her father. Mr. Drew was sitting at the kitchen table paying bills.

"Daddy, Daddy?" Nancy asked. "Did you ever hear of the Abominable Snowman?"

"Sure have," Mr. Drew said. "I think he's also called Bigfoot."

"Bigfoot!" Nancy gasped under her breath.

She remembered the footprints they saw in the snow. They were big. Very big!

"Daddy, can I please call George?" Nancy asked. "It's about our case."

"Sure," Mr. Drew said. "Just don't stay on too long."

Nancy ran back to the den. She picked up the phone and quickly dialed George's number.

"Fayne residence and catering service," George said as she answered. "Who is speaking—"

"George, call Bess!" Nancy cut in. "We're going to the Museum of Natural History first thing tomorrow!"

That night Nancy tossed and turned in bed. She couldn't stop wondering if the snowman they had seen in the park was the Abominable Snowman. Or Bigfoot!

Maybe I should have taken a picture too, Nancy said as she slowly drifted off to sleep.

The next day was Friday. Right after breakfast Hannah drove Nancy, Bess, and George to the museum. While Hannah admired an exhibit on rare gems, the girls checked out the Abominable Snowman exhibit. The director of the museum, Mr. Fauntelroy, pointed out all of the photographs.

"Are you sure that's the Abominable Snowman?" Nancy asked. "It looks more like some furry ape!"

Nancy tilted her head as she studied one of the pictures. It showed a white furry creature lumbering through the woods. His arms hung low and his feet were flat and long.

"Well, now," Mr. Fauntelroy said. His mustache wiggled as he spoke. "What did you expect the

Abominable Snowman to look like?"

George shrugged and said, "The snowman we saw in the park had a blue scarf around his neck!"

"And he was kind of cute," Bess said. "In a roly-poly way."

Mr. Fauntelroy blinked. He cracked a small smile and said, "I don't think you saw the Abominable Snowman, girls. I think you had a *Frosty* sighting!"

Nancy smiled politely as Mr. Fauntelroy laughed at his own joke. She knew they hadn't seen Frosty the Snowman. And she knew they hadn't seen Bigfoot either.

"Thanks for showing us the pictures, Mr. Fauntelroy," Nancy said. "They were very interesting."

"You're welcome!" Mr. Fauntelroy said. "And don't forget about our insect exhibit in the spring. We'll have one of the world's biggest cockroaches under glass!"

"Ew," Bess said as they walked away.

The girls joined Hannah in the gem room. She was only halfway through the exhibit.

"Why don't you girls look for your birth-stones?" she said. "There's supposed to be a giant amethyst around here."

"I think we'd rather talk about our case now, Hannah," Nancy said.

"Okay, Clue Crew," Hannah said with a smile. "Meet me outside in fifteen minutes. Stay by the entrance and don't go anywhere."

Nancy, Bess, and George bundled up in their jackets, scarves, and hats. They walked through the revolving door and stood outside on the sidewalk.

"The snowman we saw in the park wasn't the Abominable Snowman," Nancy sighed.

"I guess it's back to square one," George said.

Bess stared at the River Heights Ice-Skating Rink. It was right next to the museum.

"The ice show is tomorrow!" Bess said. "I have my costume. I know what I have to do. So why am I so nervous?"

"It's okay, Bess," Nancy said. "I'll bet even Svetlana and Alexi Dubonov are nervous about the show."

Suddenly Bess's eyes popped wide open. "Omigosh! Omigosh! Omigosh!" she cried.

"Not *that* nervous!" George said.

"No!" Bess cried. Her finger shook as she pointed over Nancy's and George's shoulders. "It's him! It's him! It's the snowman!"

Nancy and George whipped around. The snowman they had seen in the park was running across the street.

"Cheese and crackers—it is him!" George exclaimed.

Nancy stared at the snowman as his scarf flapped in the wind. In his hands were some bright pink papers.

"What are we waiting for?" George said. She started to run. "Let's go after him!"

Nancy grabbed the hem of George's jacket. "We can't!" she said. "Hannah told us to wait here!"

The girls shouted after the snowman.

"Stop!" Nancy yelled.

"Freeze!" George shouted. "I mean—thaw!"

The snowman kept dashing down River Street.

George bent down and scooped up a handful of snow. "They didn't make me pitcher on our baseball team for nothing," she said. "Stand back!"

George patted the snow into a snowball. She swung back her arm and hurled it across the street. It hit the snowman on the shoulder with a loud *thonk!*

"Got him!" George cheered.

The top part of the snowman toppled off. Nancy watched in horror as it rolled over and over on the icy ground.

"You did more than that, George!" Nancy cried. "You knocked off his head!"

ChaPTER TEN

Nice on Ice

The girls stared across the street. In place of the snowman's head was a human head. A teen-age boy's head!

"It's a costume," George said.

The boy kneeled down to pick up the pink papers.

"What goes on here?" a voice with a Russian accent demanded.

Nancy, Bess, and George turned around. Standing at the stage door of the ice rink were Svetlana and Alexi Dubonov!

"We heard noise and come out!" Alexi said. He and Svetlana wrapped themselves in their coats as they walked over to the girls.

"Bess, is everything good?" Svetlana asked.

"I think so," Bess said.

Nancy's mouth hung wide open. She couldn't believe they were actually standing next to the famous ice-skaters. Her voice shook as she pointed and said, "Um—we saw that snowman across the street. I mean we saw him before, in the park!"

Alexi looked across the street and said, "That is Lance. He hands out fliers for the show in front of the rink."

"Oh!" Bess said. "Just like those fliers we saw in the garbage can!"

"Garbage can?" Alexi and Svetlana said together.

Lance walked across the street with his snowman head under his arm. "Yo," he said. "Who threw that snowball?"

"I did," George admitted.

Nancy expected Lance to be mad, but instead he smiled.

"Wicked pitch!" Lance said with a grin. "You go, girl!"

"Thanks!" George said, grinning back.

But Alexi and Svetlana were not smiling.

"What were you doing in the park, Lance?" Alexi asked. "When you should have been giving out fliers here?"

Lance's face turned red. It wasn't from the cold!

"I didn't know I'd have to dress up like a snowman when I took the job," Lance said. "If my buds saw me like this they'd be on my case for weeks."

"But you were a great snowman," Nancy said. "You really had us fooled!"

"And there's nothing wrong with wearing a snowman suit," Bess said.

"There is if you're the star of your high-school ice hockey team," Lance said. He turned to Svetlana and Alexi. "I'm sorry about the fliers. I'll work extra late tonight to hand them out."

But Svetlana looked deep in thought. "Ice hockey?" she said. "You skate, Lance?"

"Like a pro!" Lance admitted. "The team calls me Lance the Blade!"

Svetlana turned to Nancy and George. "Do you skate too?" she asked.

"We love to skate!" Nancy said.

"I even did a figure eight once!" George said. "Well . . . it was more like a figure six. But close enough."

Svetlana turned to her husband and smiled. "Lance skate. Girls skate," she said. "Alexi—I have a huge idea!"

Nancy traded puzzled looks with Bess and George. What could it be?

"You were awesome in the ice show, Bess," Nancy said.

"And I didn't fall once!" Bess said happily.

It was Saturday night. Bess had just skated with Svetlana and Alexi in the River Heights Ice Spectacular Show. Thanks to the skating couple, Nancy and George had parts too. They wore colorful snowsuits and skated out on the ice with Lance the Snowman!

This time Lance didn't mind wearing a

snowman suit. Especially when his hockey team started cheering, "Go Blade! Go Blade! Go Blade!"

After the show the Drews, Faynes, and Marvins went to Pizza Paradise for pies all around. But Nancy, Bess, and George celebrated more than just the ice show. They celebrated one more mystery solved by the Clue Crew!

"Large pepperoni pizza with cheese!" the perky waitress with the ponytail said. She

placed the pie on the small round table the girls shared. "Enjoy your meal!"

Nancy waited for the waitress to walk away. Then she closed her eyes and began waving both hands over the pie.

"Nancy!" George whispered. Her eyes darted around to see if anyone was looking. "What are you doing?"

"I am Madame Pepperona!" Nancy said with a deep voice. "And I read pepperonis on pizza pies!"

Bess giggled and said, "So what do you see in our future, Madame Pepperona?"

Nancy opened her eyes and smiled. "Mysteries!" she said. "Lots and lots of mysteries!"

Make a Snowflake!

There's no business like snow business! But you don't have to live in a snowy state like Nancy, Bess, and George to have fun with flakes. Just get crafty—and make your own!

Beaded snowflakes are pretty and fun to make!

*You will need:

Gold, white, or silver pipe cleaners (three
   for each snowflake)
One sunburst bead for the middle of
   each snowflake
Lots of beads—white, clear,
   crystal, or pastel
Glue and glitter
String
(*You can pick up most snowflake supplies
at a local crafts store!)

Ready, Set, Snow . . .

Take three pipe cleaners and your sunburst bead. Stick the pipe cleaners through the hole of the sunburst bead so they are the same length on each side of the bead. Spread the pipe cleaners out to make the frame of the snowflake. Add beads to pipe cleaners. When pipe cleaner is filled with beads, fold the end into the last bead. For extra shimmer, dot your snowflake with glue and sprinkle on glitter! No two snowflakes are alike, so go wild with different shapes and designs!

To hang up your snowflake, tie a thin or see-through string to the top. Or to make a sassy "snow mobile" for your room, hang a bunch of snowflakes on the frame of a coat hanger!

A Frosty Fact!

All snowflakes may be different, but they have one thing in common: They all have six sides and six points!

Read all the books in the

Blast to the Past

series!

HUNGRY FOR MORE MAD SCIENCE?

CATCH UP WITH FRANNY AS SHE CONDUCTS OTHER EXPERIMENTS!